WAITING

KEVIN HENKES

GREENWILLOW BOOKS
An Imprint of HarperCollinsPublishers

Waiting. Copyright © 2015 by Kevin Henkes. All rights reserved. Printed in the United States of America. For information address HarperCollins Children's Books, a division of HarperCollins Publishers, 195 Broadway, New York, NY 10007. www.harpercollinschildrens.com. Brown ink, watercolor paint, and colored pencils were used to prepare the full-color art. The text type is 23-point Tarzana Wide. Library of Congress Cataloging-in-Publication Data. Henkes, Kevin, author, illustrator. Waiting / Kevin Henkes. pages cm. "Greenwillow Books." Summary: An owl, puppy, bear, rabbit, and pig wait for marvelous things to happen. ISBN 978-0-06-236843-0 (trade ed.)— ISBN 978-0-06-236844-7 (lib. ed.) [1. Waiting (Philosophy)—Fiction. 2. Animals—Fiction.] I. Title. PZ7.H389Wai 2015 [E]—dc23 2014030560 16 17 18 19 WOR 10 9 8   First Edition

 Greenwillow Books

For Paul and Ruiko

There were five of them.

And they were waiting. . . .

The owl with spots was waiting for the moon.

The pig with the umbrella was waiting for the rain.

The bear with the kite was waiting for the wind.

The puppy on the sled was waiting for the snow.

The rabbit with stars

wasn't waiting for anything in particular.

He just liked to look out the window and wait.

When the moon came up,
the owl was happy.
It happened a lot.

When the rain came down,
the pig was happy.
The umbrella kept her dry.

When the wind blew,
the bear was happy.
The kite flew high and far.

When it finally snowed,
the puppy was happy.
He'd waited a very long time.

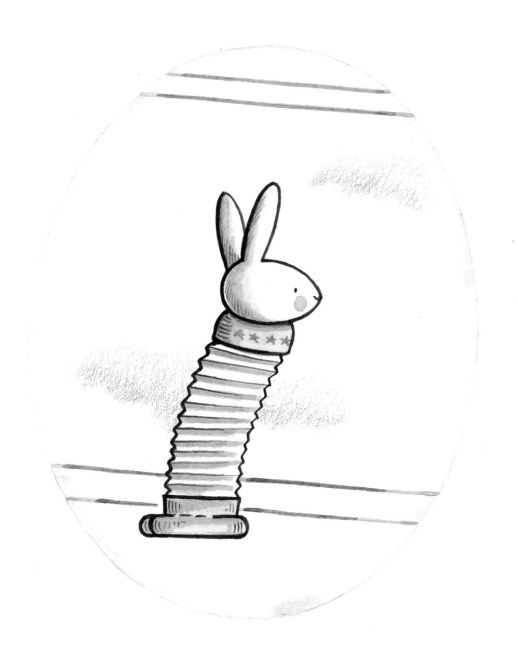

The rabbit was happy just looking out the window.

Sometimes one or the other of them went away,

but he or she always came back.

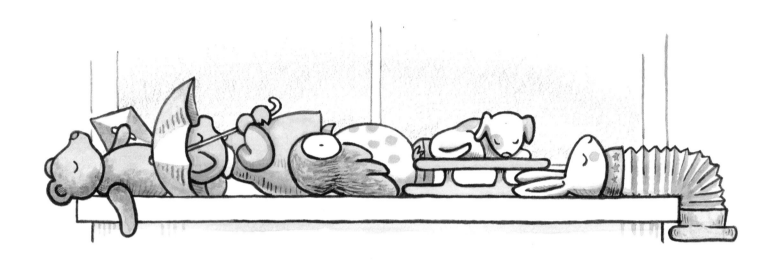

Sometimes they slept.

But mostly they waited.

Sometimes gifts appeared.

Once a visitor arrived from far away.

He stayed a while,

then

he

left

and

never

returned.

They saw many wonderful, interesting things. . . .

And, of course,
there was always
the moon
and the rain
and the wind
and the snow
to keep them happy.

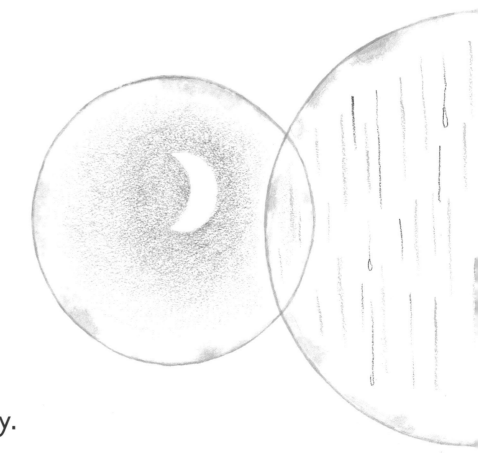

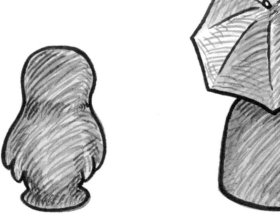

One day a cat with patches joined them.

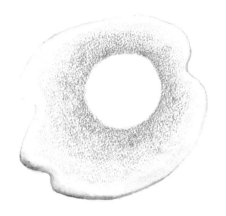

Was she waiting for the moon?

No.

Was she waiting for the rain?

No.

Was she waiting for the wind?

No.

Was she waiting for the snow?

No.

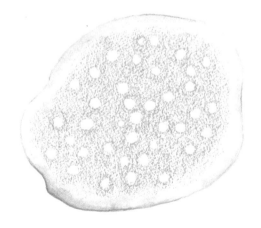

She didn't seem to be waiting
for anything in particular—

Oh, but she was!

Now, there were ten of them.

And they were happy together,

waiting to see what would happen next.